Sweet Music in Harlem

by Debbie A. Taylor * illustrated by Frank Morrison

Lee & Low Books Inc. * New York

Acknowledgement
Special thanks to the Art Kane Archives for the use of the historic photo,
Harlem 1958, featured on the last page of this book.

Manufactured in China

Book Design by David Neuhaus/NeuStudio
Book Production by The Kids at Our House

The text is set in Senza Medium
The illustrations are rendered in acrylic

10 9 8 7 6 5 4 3 2 1
First Edition

Library of Congress Cataloging-in-Publication Data
Taylor, Debbie A.
Sweet music in Harlem / by Debbie A. Taylor ; illustrated by Frank Morrison.— 1st ed.
p. cm.
Summary: C.J., who aspires to be as great a jazz musician as his uncle, searches for Uncle Click's hat
in preparation for an important photograph and inadvertently gathers some of the greatest musicians
of 1950s Harlem to join in on the picture.
ISBN 1-58430-165-1
[1. Musicians—Fiction. 2. Jazz—Fiction. 3. Harlem (New York, N.Y.)—History—20th century—Fiction.
4. Uncles—Fiction. 5. Lost and found possessions—Fiction. 6. Photographs—Fiction.
7. African Americans—Fiction.] I. Morrison, Frank, ill. II. Title.
PZ7.T21238Sw 2004
[E]—dc21   2003008994

To my mother, Rosetta, my daughters, Erika and Elaina,
and to my husband, Charles

—D.A.T.

To my favorite quartet . . .

Nyree	Tyreek	Nia	Nasir
on	on	on	on
bass	sax	vocals	trumpet

—F.M.

"C.J., where can my hat be?" called Uncle Click from the bathroom. "That photographer from *Highnote* magazine will be out front in an hour, and I've got to look good. It's not every day a Harlem trumpet player gets his picture taken."

C. J. smiled at the old poster on the wall. A young
Uncle Click with a snappy black beret blew a gleaming trumpet.
C. J. looked at that poster every morning and dreamed of standing
onstage, blowing his own sweet music for a roomful of admiring folks.

During the four years he had lived with Uncle Click, C. J. had learned to
hold his clarinet just right, to practice every day, and to keep a penny in his
shoe for good luck. When he blew out the candles on his birthday cake next
week, he'd wish that one day his own picture would be on a poster too. But
for now C. J. just tried to make his notes ring out clear and strong from
his dented, secondhand clarinet.

Uncle Click chuckled as he walked into the room. "Those were the days," he said, nodding at the poster. "Back then I played the meanest trumpet in Harlem. Now all I do is lose things."

"Don't worry, Uncle Click. I'll find your hat," C. J. said. "Where could you have left it?"

"Well," said Uncle Click as he looked behind the couch. "Last night I stopped at the barbershop and the diner. Later on I jammed at the Midnight Melody Club . . ." Uncle Click's voice trailed off as he searched under the cushion of his favorite chair.

When music was on Uncle Click's mind, he forgot everything else. He could have left his hat anywhere, and there wasn't much time to find it.

C. J. ran down the street. The striped pole outside Garlic's Barbershop glistened like a candy cane. Inside, the place buzzed as everyone talked at once. At Garlic's neighborhood news traveled faster than a subway train speeding downtown.

"Did you see that Kansas City drummer cut loose at the Midnight Melody last night?" one of the men shouted.

"Yeah, he was cool, but it sure was hot in there!" someone else replied.

Mr. Garlic talked louder than anyone. A toothpick jutting from the corner of his mouth bounced up and down as he scolded a fidgety customer.

"Mr. Garlic," C. J. called, but no one heard him.

"Mr. Garlic!" C. J. said again, louder.

The barber finally spotted C. J. and smiled. "Looky here, it's my favorite young jazzman. Mark my words, he'll be a headliner soon! What can I do for you, C. J.?"

"A photographer from *Highnote* magazine is coming soon," C. J. blurted out," and Uncle Click lost his hat. Did he leave it here?"

"Your uncle didn't leave his hat, but he did leave this," said Mr. Garlic, holding up a shiny watch. "When Click blows his horn that barber pole spins, but he *is* a little forgetful."

C. J. thanked Mr. Garlic and slipped the watch into his pocket.

"You say some photographer is coming from *Highnote?*" Mr. Garlic said. "Well, a photo without Big Charlie Garlic wouldn't be much of a picture, right folks?"

As C. J. hurried away, he could hear the people in the barbershop buzzing about the photographer. "I've got to find that hat," C. J. muttered to himself.

C. J. rushed around the corner and into the jam-packed Eat and Run Diner. Just inside the door he jumped back as a waitress zipped past, balancing plates of ham and eggs on one arm and home fries and sausage on the other.

The waitress grinned at C. J., her apron still swaying from her dash across the room. "Hey, C. J.," she said.

"Hi, Mattie Dee," said C. J. "Did Uncle Click leave his hat here? A photographer from *Highnote* magazine is coming to take his picture in a few minutes, and Uncle Click needs his hat."

"Honey, Click didn't leave his hat, but he did leave this," said Mattie Dee. She pulled a handkerchief from her pocket and dropped it into C. J.'s hand.

"Your uncle leaves his things all over Harlem, but when he wails on his trumpet, the saltshakers bounce! And if you keep practicing, one day you'll make them bounce too."

"Thanks for the hankie, Mattie Dee," C. J. said.

"Did you say a photographer from *Highnote* is coming?" Mattie Dee asked. "I'd love to be in the picture—especially if I can stand right next to your handsome uncle."

As C. J. left the diner, he could hear Mattie Dee telling her customers about the photographer. "But I've still got to find Uncle Click's hat!" C. J. moaned.

C. J. raced down the block, then bounded down the stairs of the Midnight Melody Club. Even though the club was closed, eight musicians were crowded onto the small stage, playing as if it were still show time. The bass player's eyes glistened as he plucked his instrument. The vibraphone player tapped the keys with his eyes closed.

"C. J.!" the drummer shouted without losing the beat. "We're saving a spot for you here. I reckon you'll be joining us in a few years."

A woman strolled toward C. J. from the back of the club. She didn't seem to notice that it wasn't nighttime. She still wore a fancy dress, and rings glittered on her fingers.

"Miss Alma!" C. J. called. "A photographer from *Highnote* magazine is coming to take Uncle Click's picture, and he can't find his hat. Did he leave it onstage last night?"

Canary Alma shook her head. "Your uncle didn't leave his hat here, but he did leave this," she said, and plucked a bow tie from the piano bench. "He's forgetful, but when Click blows his trumpet the wallpaper curls."

C. J. thanked Canary Alma and slid the tie over his wrist.

"A photographer from *Highnote!*" Canary Alma exclaimed, smoothing her dress. "My face next to your uncle's will give that photo a touch of class."

C. J.'s shoulders drooped as he left the Midnight Melody Club. He didn't want to disappoint Uncle Click, but he just couldn't find that hat anywhere.

C. J. dragged his feet up the steps of the brownstone where his uncle waited. A lump like a sour ball wedged in C. J.'s throat.

"Uncle Click," C. J. said. "I didn't find your hat, but I did find these." He held out the watch, the handkerchief, and the bow tie.

Uncle Click looked at C. J., and a huge smile spread across his face. "Looks like you found something else too," he said, pointing behind C. J.

C. J. turned around. Big Charlie Garlic, Mattie Dee, and Canary Alma were walking down the street toward them. But they weren't alone! They were followed by men from the barbershop, people from the diner, and musicians from the Midnight Melody Club. There were also folks C. J. had never seen before and people he'd only seen on posters or record covers.

"Hey, Click," called Charlie Garlic. "You sure know how to gather a crowd."

"Wasn't me," said Uncle Click, winking at C. J.

C. J. could hardly believe his eyes. Here were some of the greatest musicians and singers in Harlem. It was like seeing the sun, the moon, and the stars all shining at once.

"Your nephew drew a crowd without even blowing a note!" said Charlie Garlic. "He won't have any trouble packing them in at the Apollo in a few years."

"I've never seen so many jazzy folks in one place, and right in front of my very own home!" said Uncle Click, a twinkle in his eyes. "This really is something special. Who needs a hat to appreciate that?"

"The photographer's here!" someone yelled.

Everyone scrambled to get a good spot on the steps. There were so many people, some ended up sitting on the curb and standing on the sidewalk.

The photographer laughed from behind his camera. "Guess I'd better use a wider lens!" he called.

As the photographer adjusted his camera, the crowd settled into position for the picture.

"Smile!" the photographer finally shouted, and then *POP!*, a bright light flashed.

Laughter and clapping filled the air.

That night as C. J. lay in bed, light from the hallway crept into his room. Uncle Click stood in the doorway with a large box wrapped in bright red paper.

"I know your birthday's not until next week," said Uncle Click, "but I wanted to give you this before all the magic of today wears off."

C. J. opened the box and lifted out a black case. His eyes widened as he raised the lid. Inside, nestled in velvet, was a brand new clarinet.

"It's perfect!" C. J. said, cradling the horn gently in his hands.

C. J. hugged his uncle tightly. Then he noticed something else in the box. "Uncle Click, your hat!"

"Well, look at that!" said Uncle Click. "It must have fallen in there last night when I was wrapping your present."

"You know, a jazzman like you is going to need a good hat," said Uncle Click as he placed the beret neatly on C. J.'s head. "Besides, I'm getting used to not wearing one."

C. J. adjusted the hat and put the clarinet to his lips. He started to blow while his fingers danced over the keys. Uncle Click beamed and nodded to the beat as C. J.'s own sweet music rang out clear and strong for the most admiring audience in all of Harlem.

Author's Note

Sweet Music in Harlem was inspired by a photograph on a T-shirt my husband was wearing one day. In the photograph a crowd of famous jazz musicians poses on the steps of a brownstone in Harlem, New York, while children sit on the curb. I wondered who those children were and what they might have thought about seeing all those people gathered on their street.

Months later, on the way to a hotel in St. Louis, I passed nightclubs, restaurants, and streets with jazz-related names. They reminded me of that picture of jazz musicians. As I sat in the hotel eating breakfast the next morning, the plot of the story evolved clearly. A boy named C. J. started racing through Harlem, trying to find his uncle's missing hat in time for a photo shoot for a jazz magazine.

The picture on that shirt was taken in 1958 by Art Kane, a young photographer on his first assignment for *Esquire* magazine. He had invited some musicians to a photo shoot in Harlem, not knowing if anyone would show up. Magically, the news spread quickly, and fifty-seven of the greatest men and women of jazz gathered, as well as some curious neighborhood children!   —D.T.

The jazz greats in the historic photograph above are numbered for your reference: 1. Hilton Jefferson; 2. Benny Golson; 3. Art Farmer; 4. Art Blakey; 5. Wilbur Ware; 6. Chubby Jackson; 7. Johnny Griffin; 8. Dickie Wells; 9. Buck Clayton; 10. Taft Jordan; 11. Zutty Singleton; 12. Red Allen; 13. Tyree Glenn; 14. Sonny Greer; 15. Jimmy Jones; 16. Miff Mole; 17. Jay C. Higginbotham; 18. Charles Mingus; 19. Jo Jones; 20. Gene Krupa; 21. Osie Johnson; 22. Max Kaminsky; 23. George Wettling; 24. Bud Freeman; 25. Pee Wee Russell; 26. Buster Bailey; 27. Jimmy Rushing; 28. Scoville Brown; 29. Bill Crump; 30. Ernie Wilkins; 31. Sonny Rollins; 32. Gigi Gryce; 33. Hank Jones; 34. Eddie Locke; 35. Horace Silver; 36. Luckey Roberts; 37. Maxine Sullivan; 38. Joe Thomas; 39. Stuff Smith; 40. Coleman Hawkins; 41. Rudy Powell; 42. Oscar Pettiford; 43. Sahib Shihab; 44. Marian McPartland; 45. Lawrence Brown; 46. Mary Lou Williams; 47. Emmett Berry; 48. Thelonious Monk; 49. Vic Dickenson; 50. Milt Hinton; 51. Lester Young; 52. Rex Stewart; 53. J. C. Heard; 54. Gerry Mulligan; 55. Roy Eldrige; 56. Dizzy Gillespie; 57. Count Basie